DISNEP
Pot o' Gold

Written by
Guy Davis

Illustrated by
Art Mawhinney

Published by
Louis Weber, C.E.O., Publications International, Ltd.
7373 North Cicero Avenue, Lincolnwood, Illinois 60712

Ground Floor, 59 Gloucester Place, London W1U 8JJ

Customer Service: 1-800-595-8484 or customer_service@pilbooks.com

www.pilbooks.com

p i kids is a registered trademark of Publications International, Ltd

Manufactured in China.
ISBN-13: 978-1-4127-3022-8
ISBN-10: 1-4127-3022-8

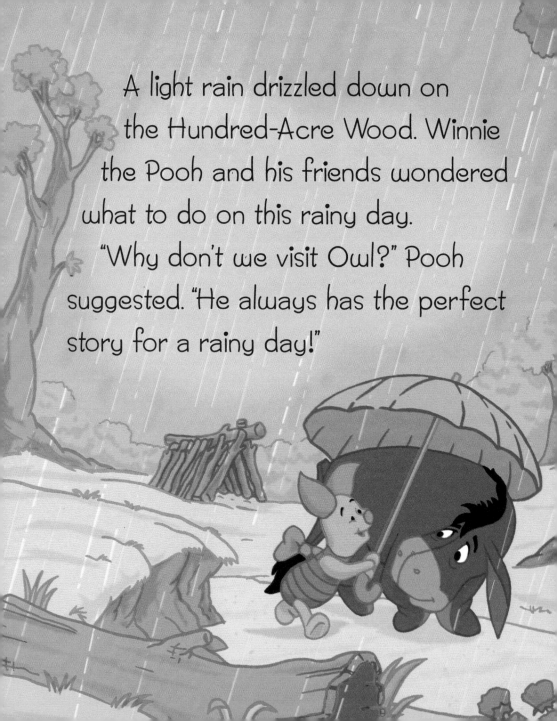

A light rain drizzled down on the Hundred-Acre Wood. Winnie the Pooh and his friends wondered what to do on this rainy day.

"Why don't we visit Owl?" Pooh suggested. "He always has the perfect story for a rainy day!"

Pooh, Piglet, Tigger, and Eeyore marched off to Owl's house. When they arrived, they asked Owl to tell them a story.

Owl agreed, of course.

"I say, my dear chaps, I have the perfect story for a rainy day like today," he said.

Owl told everyone a story about a rainbow and all of its beautiful colors—red, orange, yellow, green, blue, and violet.

"And at the end of every rainbow, that's where you'll find a pot of gold!" said Owl.

Then Tigger
noticed that the rain had
stopped. "Hoo-hoo-hoo!" he
cried suddenly, pointing outside.
"Look what I see!"

Everyone looked out Owl's
window. They saw a beautiful
rainbow arching across the sky!

Owl stayed behind to clean up, but the others decided to follow the colorful rainbow.

Tigger and Pooh bravely led the expedition deep into the woods, while Eeyore and Piglet slowly brought up the rear. Where did the rainbow end, they wondered?

Soon, they couldn't see the
rainbow for the trees! "Oh, dear,"
worried Piglet. "I believe we're lost!"
"No, we're not lost," replied Pooh.
"But I think the rainbow is."

"Don't worry, finding rainbows is what tiggers do best," said Tigger. "Because tiggers bounce!"

And with that, Tigger bounced up...and up...and up! Finally, he bounced so high, he flew above the trees.

"Hoo-hoo-hoo!" cried Tigger. "I can see our rainbow!"

Following the bouncing Tigger,
Pooh and his friends dashed out of
the dark and into a clearing.

Tigger kept bouncing along.
"Here it is," he cried. "Big as day!"

"Look!" said Piglet,
smiling. "The
rainbow ends
right at
Pooh's house!"

"That's funny," said Pooh, "I don't remember having a pot of gold."

The friends excitedly burst into Pooh's house, but they were quite surprised by what they found. Instead of a pot of gold, there was a pot of golden honey sitting in sunlight.

Tigger was very disappointed.

But Pooh wasn't disappointed in the least!

"It might not be a pot of gold," sighed Pooh, licking his paws. "But I have my honeypot, and that's the best treasure of all!"